ALLIGATOR AND THE TOOTH FAIRY

By JO-ANNA ROBERTS

Illustrated by SHANNON KINNELL

Published by

Desert Star International
PO Box 1850
Sparks, NV 89432-1850

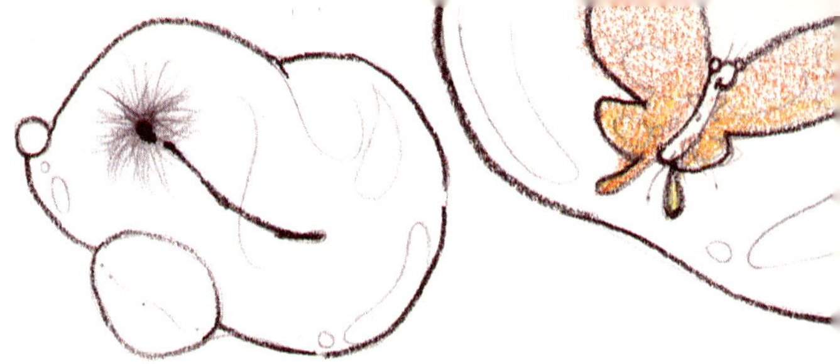

ALLIGATOR AND THE TOOTH FAIRY

Library of Congress Catalog Card Number: 90-84369
ISBN: 1-879212-00-5

Without Christ's love for me, this book would never have been possible.

This book is dedicated in memory of my mother and father. They are together again at last. I love you Mama and Daddy.

Once upon a time, deep inside the massive swamps of Alligatorville, lived a little alligator named Oliver.

Oliver was quite handsome for an alligator. All of his friends who lived in the swamps knew him as Oli.

One day, while he was playing in the swamp with his best friend Herman, they saw a boat in the distance coming toward them.

"We better hide before they see us," said Oli.

They hid themselves alongside a branch floating in the water.

The branch disguised them so well that even from a few feet away they were unable to be seen.

Inside the boat they saw a small boy and two grownups. They slowed down, then stopped along the bank to rest for a while.

"OH NO, they're stopping," cried Oli.

"That's just our luck," said Herman, "we'll be late again."

"I hope they don't stay very long," said Oli. "That's all I need is to be late again. I'll probably be grounded for life."

"I wonder why they're stopping,"

Herman whispered.

The alligators were very curious, so they swam a little closer to the boat. They could hear the little boy talking about a Tooth Fairy and how his tooth had just fallen out.

The little boy's father told him to save the tooth and put it under his pillow when they get back home.

"What the heck is a Tooth Fairy?" asked Herman.

"SHHHH," whispered Oli. "Be quiet and maybe we'll find out."

"The Tooth Fairy," said his father, "will come during the night to take it back to Toothland. She will leave you a nice surprise under your pillow."

At that moment, the father took out the oars of the boat and off they went.

When Oli and Herman came out of hiding, the only thing Oli could think about was the Tooth Fairy that the little boy's father talked about.

He wiggled a tooth of his own and said, "Look Herman. My tooth is about to come out!"

"Ah, you don't believe that stuff about the Tooth Fairy, do you?" asked Herman. "Oh come on! There's no such thing."

Oli was not convinced, he knew he couldn't say anything more to Herman about the Tooth Fairy. He wondered... if he put his tooth under his pillow, would the Tooth Fairy come visit him too? Would the Tooth Fairy take his tooth back to Toothland? Would the Tooth Fairy leave him a nice surprise?

The sun was setting over the swamp. Oli and Herman knew they were late and that it was past their time to go home. (In fact, it was much later than they thought.)

"I'm in big trouble!" cried Herman. "We'd better run home."

"Yeah," agreed Oli. "I'll see you tomorrow."

Both Oli and Herman took off in different directions and ran home.

When Oli came through the door, he found his mother had been very worried because he was not home on time and she did not know where he was.

First, Oli's mother hugged him because she knew he was safe. Then she scolded him saying, "Oli, this is the last time you'll come home late."

"I'm very sorry," said Oli to his mother. "I'll try very hard never to be late again."

His mother said, "Okay Oli, I'll give you one more chance. But if it ever happens again, you'll be grounded to the yard. Is that clear, son?"

Oli nodded. Then his mother smiled and said, "Now come to dinner before it gets cold."

At the dinner table, he asked his mother about the Tooth Fairy. She answered, "Oh Oli, there's no such thing as the Tooth Fairy. At least not in Alligatorville."

His sisters laughed and said, "This time Oli, you are REALLY being silly."

But he didn't pay any attention to his sisters' laughter. He truly believed there was a Tooth Fairy, and that one day she would come visit him.

That night, while Oli was brushing his teeth before bed time, his loose tooth fell out.

Oli rinsed his mouth, picked up his tooth, and ran to his bed.

He lifted up his pillow and put the tooth underneath it.

Oli said goodnight to his family and ran back to his room.

Oli clasped his hands in front of him, closed his eyes, and said, "Oh PLEASE TOOTH FAIRY, I know you're real, so please come and visit me tonight." Then, he jumped into bed.

Oli laid awake in his bed and waited and waited. He stared out his bedroom window, waiting for the Tooth Fairy to come visit him.

After a long time passed, Oli began to think that his mother may be right. Maybe there really isn't a Tooth Fairy.

Deep down in his heart, Oli knew there really was a Tooth Fairy.

The night was getting darker and darker, and the time was getting later and later. Oli just laid there, staring out the window.

Oli was almost asleep when he saw something that made his eyes grow the size of baseballs. He sat up in bed and rubbed his eyes.

Standing beside his window was the most beautiful woman he had ever seen. Her hair was as gold as moonlight and wavy like the river. Her skin was as white as snow. Her eyes were like two stars in the heavens, and she had two wings on her back. They were prettier than any butterfly wings he had ever seen.

Then the Tooth Fairy said in a voice as soft as cotton, "Hello, Oli. I'm the Tooth Fairy, and I've come to take your fallen tooth back to Toothland."

"You really are the Tooth Fairy!" cried Oli.

He was very excited because he knew the Tooth Fairy was real even after his sisters had laughed at him, and his mother and Herman told him there was no such person.

"I have come to you because you truly believe in me. When you believe in something with all your heart," said the Tooth Fairy, "it will come true."

Then she reached under Oli's pillow, took his tooth, and said, "Now close your eyes and sleep. In the morning you will find your surprise."

"I'll see you again when you lose your next tooth," said the Tooth Fairy, then she disappeared.

The next morning, when Oli woke up, he thought the Tooth Fairy's visit was only a dream.

He remembered her saying that he would find his surprise in the morning.

Now it was morning, so where was his surprise? He put his hand under his pillow and pulled out a beautiful golden watch.

"It really wasn't a dream!" shouted Oli. "The Tooth Fairy is real!" He ran out of his room to show his mother and sisters his new golden watch that the Tooth Fairy had brought him during the night.

"Show me exactly where you found this beautiful new watch, Oli," his mother said.

Oli lead his mother by the hand back to his bedroom and to his pillow.

On the floor beside the window, his mother noticed the fine layer of glistening stardust left behind by the Tooth Fairy.

Oli told her what had happened during the night -- how the Tooth Fairy had taken his tooth, and how pretty she was.

Oli looked at his sisters, who were trying to pull out their own teeth. They wanted to be visited by the Tooth Fairy and get a surprise also.

He just laughed and told his sisters, "It's not enough to pull your teeth out. If you truly believe in something, believe truly with all your heart... it will come true."

Oli's mother kissed him, held him tightly, and said, "With this beautiful new watch, you'll never be late again." Oli couldn't wait to tell Herman. He knew he would see the Tooth Fairy again, because he truly believed.